Do NOT LET YOUR DRAGON SPREAD GERMS

WRITTEN BY JULIE GASSMAN   ILLUSTRATED BY ANDY ELKERTON

Once in a while, you might get a cough,
or a case of the sniffles, or feel a bit off.

When you're sneezy and drippy, think of others' health.
Do all that you can to keep bugs to yourself . . .

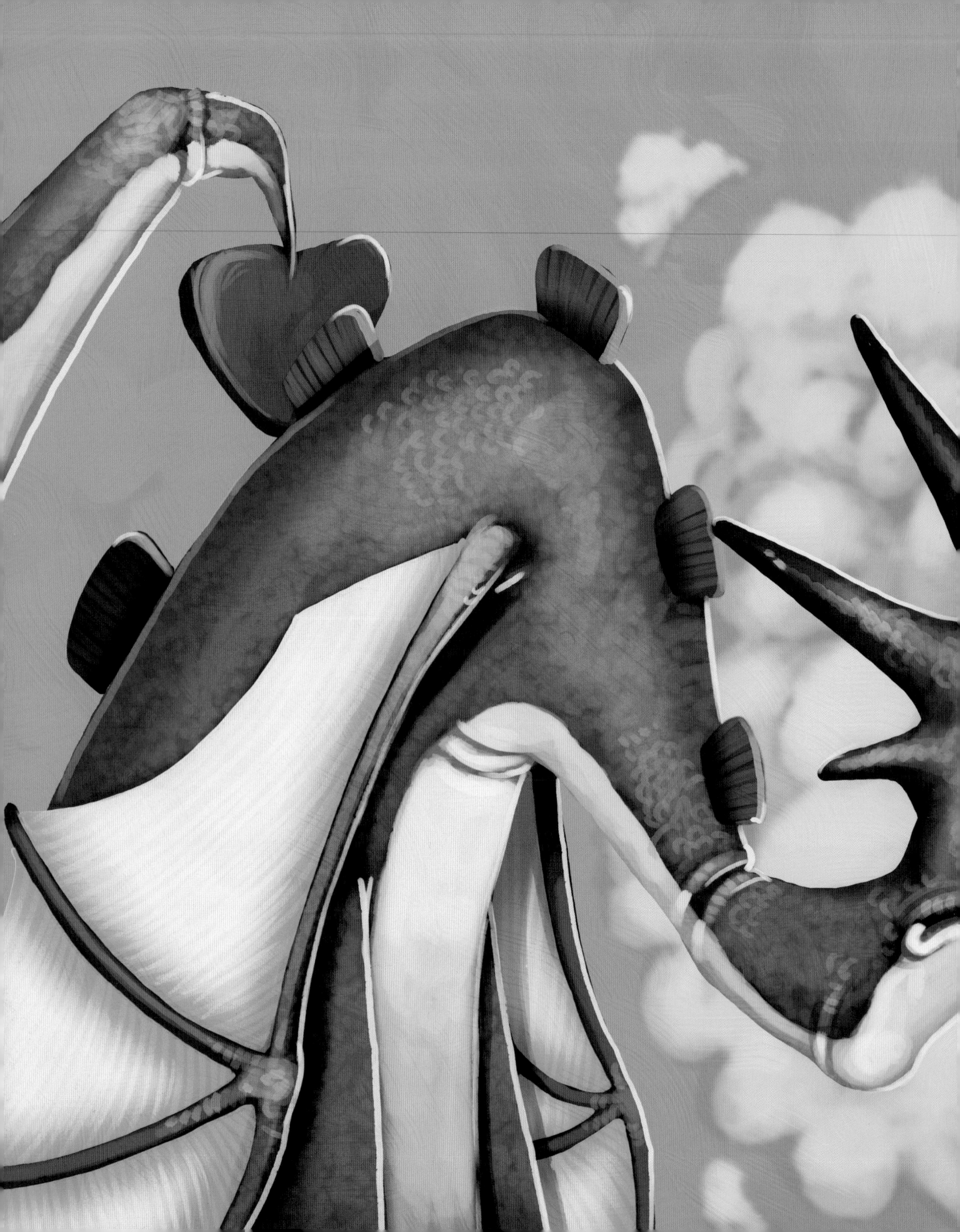

First, teach your dragon how to wash his hands right.
Get them wet, add soap, then scrub with some might.

He must lather all over for twenty seconds, at least.
For though it is tiny, a germ's a strong beast!

SO DO **NOT** LET YOUR DRAGON SPREAD GERMS!

Remind your dragon not to touch his face.
His eyes, mouth and snout are a wing-free space.

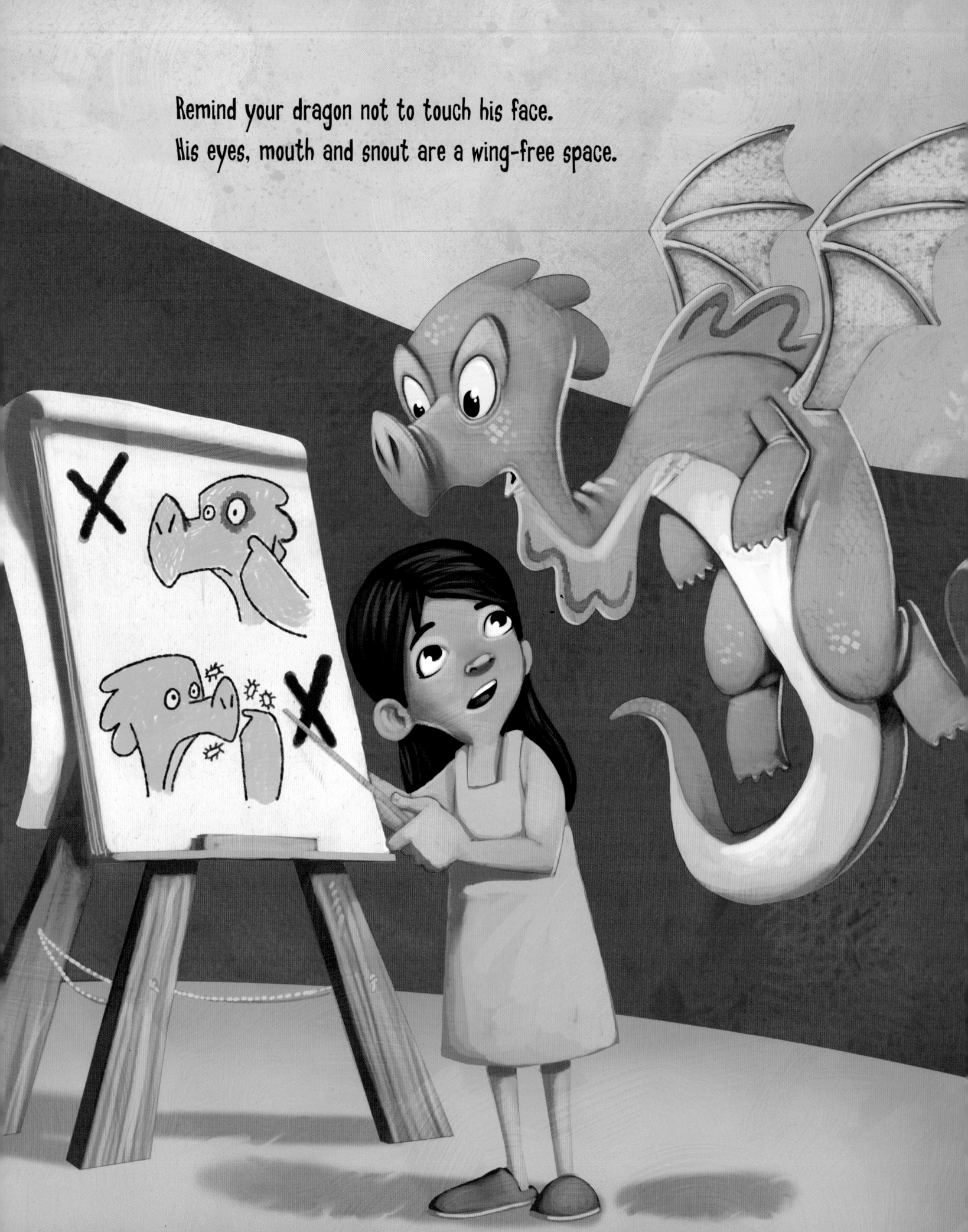

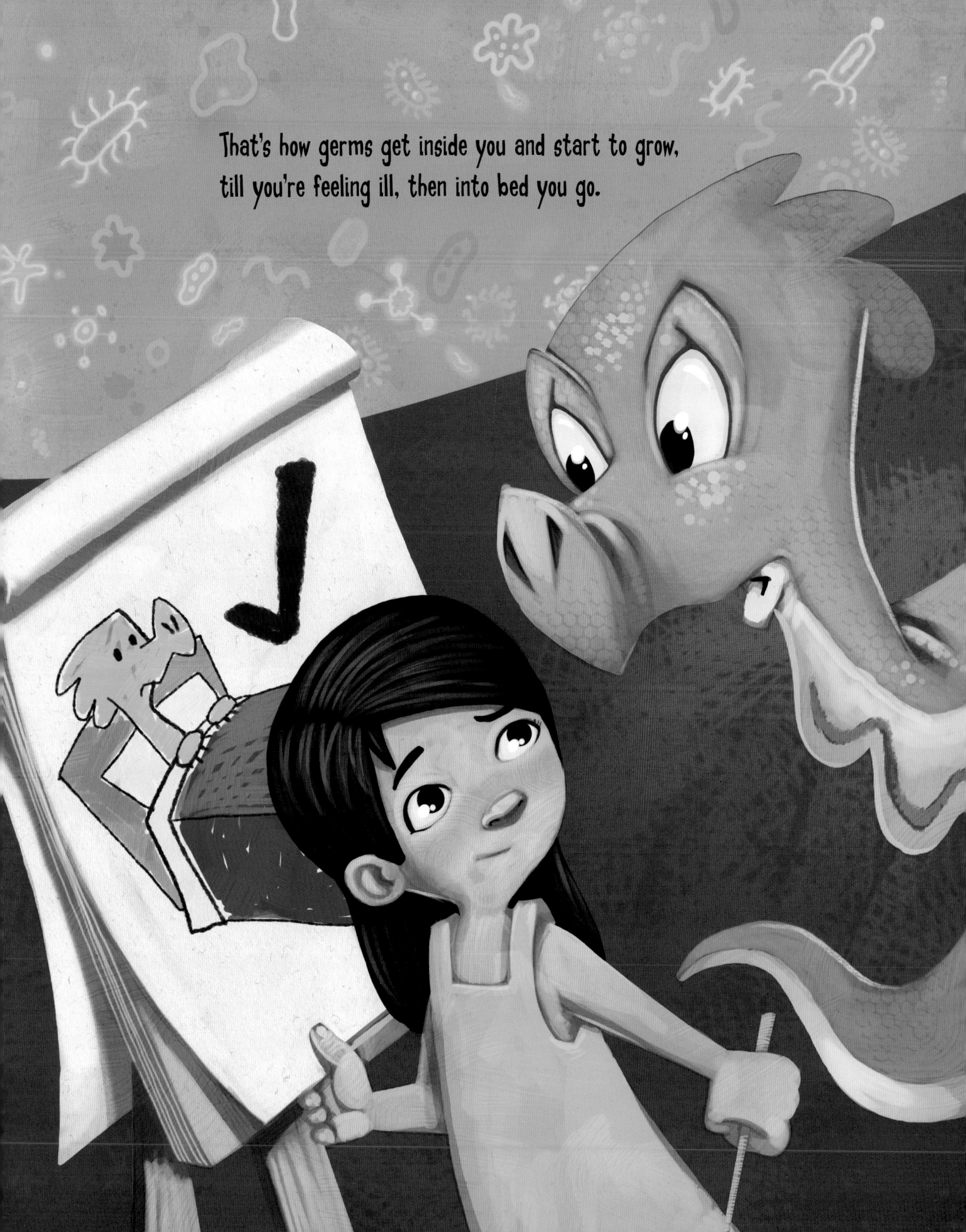

That's how germs get inside you and start to grow,
till you're feeling ill, then into bed you go.

Real dragon-germ slayers will want to wear a mask.
Listen to these rules to master the task.

Make sure you cover both the mouth and the snout.
Adjust it at the horns. Wear it each time you go out.

Your dragon might be tempted to stand way too close,
or sneeze without covering — YUCK, how gross!

He might keep giving out high-fives and hugs
and insist that his fire will kill off the bugs.

BUT DO NOT LET YOUR

DRAGON SPREAD GERMS!

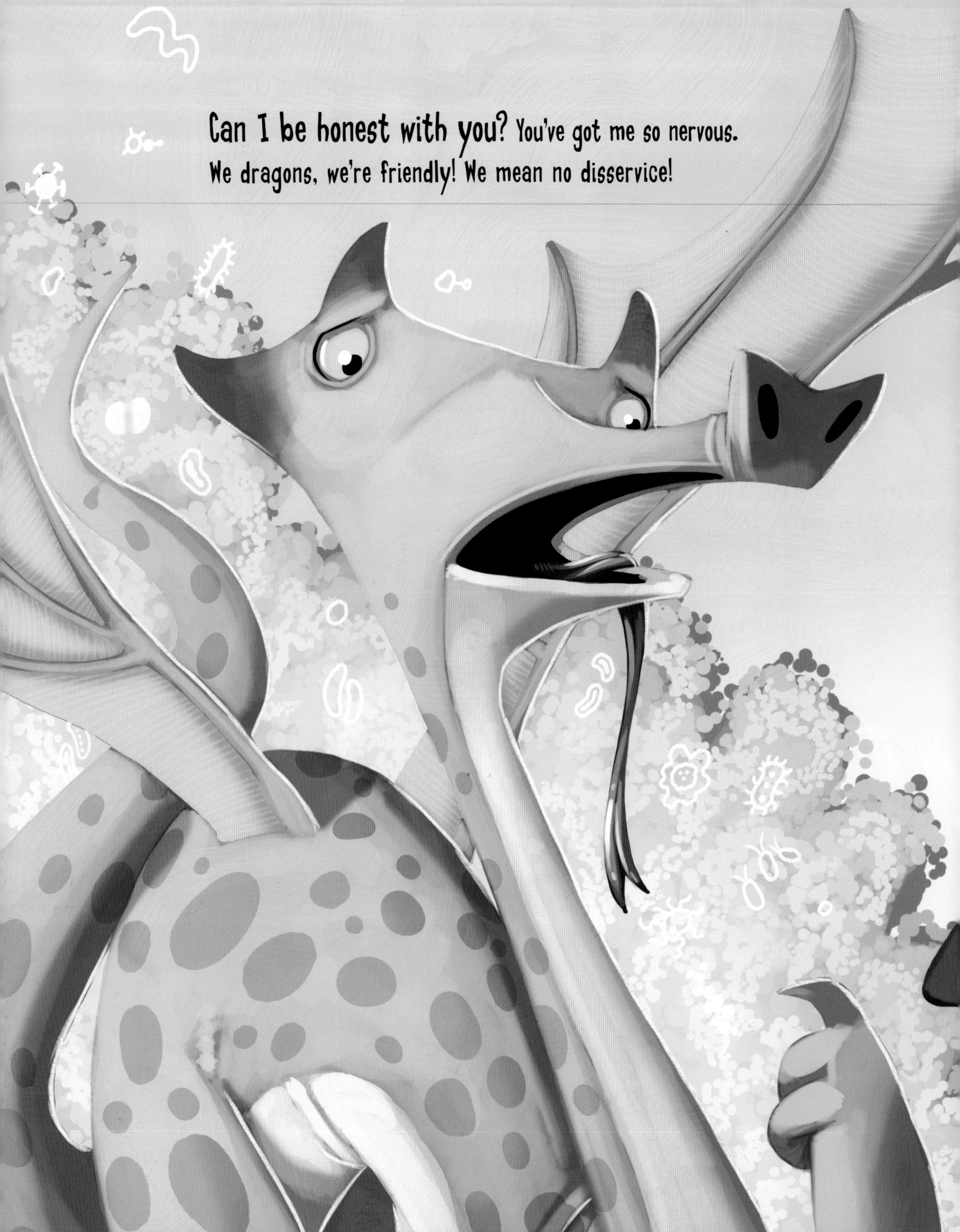

Can I be honest with you? You've got me so nervous.
We dragons, we're friendly! We mean no disservice!

We just want to play and have fun running around,
but all this germ talk, it makes us feel down.

If we sit too close, will we make our friends sad?
If we let out a sneeze, will we make our friends mad?

We don't want to make anyone squirm.
But now we're so worried about spreading our germs!

Making you worry was not my intention.
I just wanted you to pay special attention.

To keep friends and family as safe as you can,
it's always best to have a stay-healthy plan.

Be active and eat right. Get plenty of rest.
Stay at home when you're poorly, and just do your best.

Remember our chat, and all that you've learned . . .

. . . and you and your dragon won't spread any germs!

ABOUT THE AUTHOR

The youngest in a family of nine children, Julie Gassman grew up in South Dakota, USA. After college, she traded in small-town life for the world of magazine publishing in New York City. She now lives in southern Minnesota with her husband and their three children. When she's ill, she takes long naps, watches lots of TV and keeps her germs to herself as well as she can.

ABOUT THE ILLUSTRATOR

After 14 years as a graphic designer, Andy Elkerton decided to go back to his illustrative roots as a children's book illustrator. Since 2002 he has produced work for picture books, educational books, advertising and toy design. Andy has worked for clients all over the world. He currently lives in a small tourist town on the west coast of Scotland with his wife and three children.

Raintree is an imprint of Capstone Global Library Limited, a company incorporated in England and Wales having its registered office at 264 Banbury Road, Oxford, OX2 7DY – Registered company number: 6695582

www.raintree.co.uk
myorders@raintree.co.uk

Designed by Nathan Gassman

ISBN: 978 1 3982 0748 6

British Library Cataloguing in Publication Data
A full catalogue record for this book is available from the British Library.

Printed and bound in India.